NUCLEAR CORONAVIRUS ZOMBIES DUOLOGY

Volume 1: Nuclear War

Volume 2: Apocalypse World

Maximus Williams

DISCLAIMER:

This is a work of fiction. Names, characters, businesses, places, events, locales, and incidents are either the products of the author's imagination or used in a fictitious manner. Any resemblance to actual persons, living or dead, or actual events is purely coincidental.

This book's story and characters are fictitious. The characters involved are wholly imaginary.

This fiction short story book may contain scenes of violence, cussing, and graphic scenes that may be objectionable to some.

This book is designed to provide entertainment purposes only to our readers. It is sold with the understanding that the publisher is not engaged to render any type of psychological, legal, or any other kind of professional advice. The content of each article is the sole expression and opinion of its author, and not necessarily that of the publisher. No warranties or guarantees are expressed or implied by the publisher's choice to include any of the content in this volume. Neither the publisher nor the individual author(s) shall be liable for any physical, psychological, emotional, financial, or commercial damages, including, but not limited to, special, incidental, consequential, or other damages. Our views and rights are the same: You are responsible for your own choices, actions, and results.

We are not advisors and we recommend you consult with a professional before making any serious decisions.

I assume no responsibility or liability for any consequences resulting directly or indirectly from any action or inaction taken as a result of following content contained on this site or in any linked materials. I do not accept any legal liability or responsibility for any injury, loss, or damage incurred by the use of, or reliance upon, or interpretation of any content contained on this book or in any linked materials.

This book is not medical advice. The content in this book is not intended or implied to be a substitute for professional medical advice, diagnosis or treatment.

CONTENTS

VOLUME 1: NUCLEAR WAR

NUCLEAR CORONAVIRUS ZOMBIES

Volume 1: Nuclear War

I was on the bus going around my normal day and I was tired after I got off work. As the bus continued to travel across the inclined city overpass, people sitting around me kept talking about the tensions between the countries, the pandemic viruses, and how there might be a nuclear war. I was too tired to care, and I didn't believe any of it.

This odd woman kept trying to hit on me and kept rambling about her life, she laughed "I already got the coronavirus and all the variants, but I don't care. I'm alright. My name is Karen by the way."

I took a step away and kept my distance from Karen, I didn't want to catch any of her viruses, nor did I find her attractive.

I took a seat away from all the weird people on the bus as I slowly took my bottle of whiskey out of the folded brown paper bag and slowly sipped on it to relieve my stress.

I took another swig out of my whiskey, and then an explosion from far away was heard. Everyone panicked and looked out the window, from afar I could see the nuclear mushroom cloud. The mushroom cloud looked like a speck from our window since it seemed so far away.

Bystanders loudly yelled, "Nuclear bomb! Everyone duck under!" I felt the blast wave and the bus started swerving.

The bus continued to swerve, and I saw people getting burned and then having a chemical reaction to the radiation.

I took cover on the floor behind the seats and used my briefcase to shield myself against the exploding glass. My left arm got a bit burned from the radiation of the blast, but I glanced over to the other end of the bus, and I saw Karen having a chemical reaction with the blast and she started biting everyone around her.

I wasn't sure if I was just drunk but everything was

real, "Fuck, Karen's virus mutated her into a nuclear coronavirus zombie."

It was a chain effect, each passenger in the frontend of the bus would just keep biting passengers and I said to myself, "Fuck this is real. It's because of the coronavirus or the vaccine combined with the nuclear radiation."

I knew that I needed to survive and so I grabbed my pocket knife from the side of my belt as I continued to sit in the back of the bus as the front side of the swerving bus was getting infected.

I knew I needed to get help from the rest of the people in the back, but they had a distinct snobby look. I said to myself, "Damn, these nerdy squares need to stop looking at their phones asking for help."

I exclaimed from the top of my lungs, "I need help here. We're a fucking team. Otherwise, we're all going to fucking die right now. No cops are around to help us. We need to fight back fucking right now."

I tried getting the unaffected remaining people in the middle section to come to the back side by yelling at them, since most of the front side had been infected, but it seemed too late. Too many were already infected.

I raised my knife up to get ready to attack zombies. Karen, who had already turned into a nuclear coronavirus zombie, leaned in trying to bite me, but I kicked her in the shin and then I tried using my knife to stab her throat, but I hesitated and froze because my thoughts of her woman human face popped up in my memory.

Before Karen could take a bite into me, a man from behind, came and stabbed her throat with a pair of scissors. Blood came gushing out of her neck and she fell to the floor. I was disgusted by the blood, but I needed to enter survival mode.

Three more men from behind then came forward with their briefcases which were good because the briefcases served as a protection.

We used our briefcases as a shield to continuously shield ourselves and then attacked back as the other zombies came for us. It was a simple defense tactic to defend and attack. Even though I was a civilian, I had taken some self-defense courses back in college.

The bus kept swerving because the driver had already been infected. I shouted, "The bus is going out of control. We got to keep kicking them in their weak radiation burned shins and continue stabbing them." I had dress shoes on, but the butt of my shoe was hard so I used my hands to grab onto the top of the handrails on the top of the bus and kicked down the zombies. As they fell, we would slice their throat with our knives or scissors.

The three other men also hit the zombies with their briefcases.

There was blood all over everywhere but I needed

to go get to the driver's seat so our bus wouldn't crash but it was too late. The bus abruptly smashed into the center divider and all of us started tumbling around. I grabbed my suitcase and put it against my head for protection hoping I wouldn't be knocked unconscious.

I laid there on the upside-down bus awakening from my unconscious state of mind wanting to move, but unable to. My body was in extreme pain, but I had to get up before I get bit from the zombies.

I could smell smoke coming out of the flipped over bus. I saw zombies crawling over with their missing legs from the crash. Everyone including the three men that helped me fight were all infected.

I immediately crawled out of the smashed windows, but I screamed in pain with every move I made with my bruised-up body.

After I crawled out of the window, I limped then made a run for it. Zombies were everywhere. I had to find shelter so I kept looking as I was frantically ran with my limped leg. A gun store with with armed men was in plain sight. I shouted, "Let me in! I'm good. I'm not infected!" The didn't move an inch, but instead they pointed their guns at me. I screamed again, "I'm not infected!"

One of the armed men moved the barrel towards my forehead, and responded to me, "We're closed off. We're not letting anyone in. Get the fuck out of our place." I responded, "I don't have time to debate. There are zombies right behind me." The armed man looked at me straight in the eyes, "I don't care."

I eventually looked to the right of my shoulder and found a convenience store. I knew there had to be some people or even if there weren't people in it, there had to be medicine in the store.

I needed to disinfect my wounds or pressure it otherwise I would keep bleeding. So, I opened the door, and it was just a father and a son with their shotguns.

The man hesitantly said, "Are you infected?" I responded, "No, I just need shelter. I just need to stay here, and I need some medication." I then blacked out.

I woke up with bandages all over me laying in the back room of the convenience store. The father and son had my hands tied in case I turned into a zombie.

I said, "Well, I need to be here for a while. There are zombies surrounded outside and everywhere around the whole street." For some reason, the zombies didn't know we were here. The lights were off, and the doors were locked.

The father whispered, "We're safe in here for now but we got to keep the lights off. You were right, you are not infected. You can stay here if you'd like. This is our home, for now, we have food and medication but when it comes down to it. I will need your help to fight off the zombies. You seem like a pretty fit guy."

The store has become my home, and I had a new family. My only concern was if the zombies attacked, would we be able to defend ourselves?

VOLUME 2: APOCALYPSE WORLD

NUCLEAR CORONAVIRUS ZOMBIES

Volume 2: Apocalypse World

Deadly screaming zombies have taken over the chaotic world plagued by nuclear wars, viruses, variants, and unapproved vaccines. The dusty air lingering was the outcome of an abrupt nuclear bomb blast which caused a chemical reaction between the radiation and the infected people which caused them to turn into Nuclear Coronavirus Zombies.

After I survived the nuclear bomb blast, I was hiding out in a dimly lit family convenience store with a sluggish bearded man and his skinny malnourished son. The explosion from the nuclear blast had caused a lot of building wood remnants to land in front of the convenience store parking lot thus allowing the store to be slightly hidden behind the remains.

I had no family out here in this city; however, I took a deeper look into my life before the explosion and realized that all my friends and coworkers were all fake, to begin with, and our common ground was mostly to climb the corporate ladder. Now that the world was filled with zombies, I could confirm that my superficial work friends were never deeply rooted in my life and that it was mostly just working and building office status with them.

I was able to bond with this new family at the convenience store with laughter and creative methods of rolling different convenience store snacks into one to create new flavors during our survival from the zombies that plagued the outside world. The bearded dad's name was Carl and his son's name was Tim.

Years have passed quickly since I sought shelter in their store and our food supply was going to run out eventually or another risk would be if the zombies had somehow got through the iron bars shielded on the door and windows.

I was somehow confident of our safety with all the guns and ammunition that Carl had stashed in this store.

I was sleeping in my usual green sleeping bag on the floor of the store in the middle of the night when I suddenly heard a huge loud noise slamming through the front entranceway. I quickly jumped out of my sleeping bag and rushed to the front with my loaded shotgun, and I saw glass shattered on the floor along with a truck that had smashed into our doorway and walls. The wheels of the truck had fresh zombie blood dripping from all of the rubber threads. In frustration, I pointed my gun at the driver, "What the fuck did you do?"

Carl and Tim caught up as well with their guns pointed at the scared trucker as he got out of his vehicle with his hands up, "I just want some food. I don't want any harm. I tried getting in, but it was closed off. Please don't shoot."

I yelled at him, "You fucking idiot. Now, all the zombies are going to come in." I looked behind the truck and I was right. Herds of zombies had already begun climbing in behind the truck.

Before the overweight trucker could even respond to my sentence, several zombies had leaped in from behind and started biting him. The trucker's eyes quickly turned sideways as he jolted his limbs. He was no longer a human but instead a zombie. The trucker zombie then made his way towards us with his mouth wide open ready to bite us along with the herds of zombies behind him.

We emptied our explosive 24-gauge shotgun ammunition shells at the deadly zombies trying to crawl in but there were too many of them. Blood splattered throughout the store as the rounds went through the bodies of the foul-stench zombies.

Carl shouted at the top of his lungs as spit came out of his mouth with each word, "Plan B! Run to our truck."

The dusty brown truck was sitting in the back parking lot outside of the convenience store but easily seen with our mounted camera. The bulk of the zombie herd was in the front, but we knew there would still be zombies everywhere including near our truck.

We had no choice but to run towards the back door to get to the truck as the front entrance zombie herd piled in. Carl hurriedly swung open the metal back door and there we saw zombies crawling around as expected.

Carl threw his only grenade at the zombies, and we then shot through the zombies with our firearms as we inched closer to our escape truck.

We finally got to the truck and frantically hopped into the car quickly upon opening it. Carl turned on the engine and set the car into drive. I asserted, "There are zombies in front of our car and blocking our pathway."

Carl pressed his foot against the gas pedal and ran them over resulting in the thumping of the vehicle. We had to do so because we were low on ammunition.

Our front window cracked as zombies slammed against the windows. Carl sped up faster and the zombies fell off our car and we were finally distant from the zombie herd.

We haven't been out near buildings and on the roads for quite some time, so it was odd seeing other remaining buildings again. As we drove on the unoccupied streets, I was surprised to see that there were unknown flags hung on the street light poles. The nation and color of the flags were unknown to us, it seemed like a new nation had formed and had taken over.

And I thought to myself, "What the fuck is going on? Who are we governed by now?" Before seeing these flags, I initially thought the world had stopped and assumed we were the few human survivors.

We continued to drive down the abandoned empty city with newly hung nation flags and immediately, a military truck quickly stopped in front of our vehicle and turned on the megaphone addressing us with a mixed European accent, "Get out of the truck and keep your hands up."

I took a good look at these tall men dressed in camouflage, who had no expression on their faces.

One of them smirked as he lit up another cigarette.

Carl whispered to me, "Listen to me, these guys look shady, we can't let them torture us to death. We'll slowly get out of the car and then shoot them."

There were no other zombies in sight, it was just us against these people dressed in unknown camouflage military outfits.

Me, Carl, and his son slowly got out of our vehicle and then they just started shooting at us. We immediately returned fire and crossfire continued on both ends until I saw Carl and Tim get shot.

The camouflaged men also got shot. There was one remaining guy on the other side of the truck. I furiously ran closer to him and then shot at him until the shotgun shells went into his head.

I quickly looked through their vehicle to double-check if anyone was still alive, but everyone was dead.

My old truck was leaking as the crossfire had damaged the engine. I looked back to check on Carl and Tim, they were both dead.

Sounds of other vehicles could be heard coming to me from a distance. I frantically took their vehicle, but everything was in a foreign language. I couldn't read, I didn't know what language it was.

I quickly started the military truck and sped off. I

knew I had to get to a safer place.

The first thing I thought was "I need to get out of the city before another military captures me. I need to get out of here. There is no way I'll get far with the amount of ammunition that I had."

I kept driving away from the city and then my tires popped. There was a tire trap that was set up in the middle of the road. I grabbed my shotgun and before I could look to my side, there were multiple guns pointed at my face.

I shouted, "I'm dropping my gun and putting my hands up. I'll follow whatever you say."

They then immediately opened the door and pistol-whipped me.

I yelled again, "I'm not infected."

Another man pointing his firearm at me shouted at me with a heavy American country accent, "Why do you have an American accent? What are you doing in an enemy truck? Who are you?"

I responded as my cracked head bled, "I can't with you all. I am American. Born and raised. My buddies got attacked by this foreign military truck and now you guys are attacking me. I have been living in a convenience store since the nuclear attack. I have no idea what is going on."

One of the leaders of the men came and said,

"Everyone, guns down. I know him. He's my former coworker from before the zombie apocalypse. Dude, James. We're what is left of the survivors. We were attacked by foreign nations and the world had been overtaken by a combination of wars and zombies. Where have you been?"

I realized that it has been years since the nuclear bomb attacks. I squinted and looked at my fellow friend, and I quickly responded, "Shit, I can't believe our nation has been taken over by a combination of foreign countries and a nuclear blast caused the majority of the population to become zombies."

The resistance of the survivors quickly towed my foreign truck to their base hidden in the nature as I was led to a hiding spot scattered throughout the different cabins. Scattered radios and firearms were laid across tables.

I was told this was now my new home and I was to help fight to gain our nation back and also fight against the Nuclear Coronavirus Zombies.

Closing Credits:

I hope you enjoyed this short-read book. Thank you for reading one of my books. I truly enjoyed writing this book and hoped you enjoyed it. My passion for writing goes beyond the limit of the sky.

Please leave me a 5-star review, it would truly mean a lot to me.

Also check out our other zombie fiction books by Maximus Williams.

Thanks again!

The End.